Ladybird  Readers

King Arthur

Series Editor: Sorrel Pitts
Text adapted by Nicole Irving
Activities written by Catrin Morris
Illustrated by Rita Petruccioli
Chapter illustrations by Valeria Valenza

LADYBIRD BOOKS

UK | USA | Canada | Ireland | Australia
India | New Zealand | South Africa

Ladybird Books is part of the Penguin Random House group of companies
whose addresses can be found at global.penguinrandomhouse.com.
www.penguin.co.uk   www.puffin.co.uk   www.ladybird.co.uk

Penguin
Random House
UK

Text adapted from *Ladybird Classics: King Arthur* published by Ladybird Books 2015
This version published by Ladybird Books 2020
001

Copyright © Ladybird Books Ltd, 2015, 2020

Printed in China

A CIP catalogue record for this book is available from the British Library

ISBN: 978-0-241-40196-5

All correspondence to:
Ladybird Books
Penguin Random House Children's
80 Strand, London WC2R 0RL

MIX
Paper from
responsible sources
FSC
www.fsc.org   FSC® C018179

King Arthur

 To download full story audio in both British and American accents, and to complete
the listening activities at the back of the book, visit **www.ladybirdeducation.co.uk**

Contents

Characters

Arthur

King Uther Pendragon

Igraine

Sir Ector

Kay

Guinevere

Merlin

Lancelot

Morgan le Fay and her son, Mordred

CHAPTER ONE

The Old King Dies

It was very quiet inside King Uther Pendragon's castle. A few people whispered— nobody spoke loudly.

"King Uther is very ill," said the guards to people who came to the castle for news of the old king.

"King Uther is dying," people whispered. "Who will be the new king of Britain? Uther and Queen Igraine have no son."

Queen Igraine was by her husband's bed.
She was watching him with worried eyes.

"Do you feel better, dear Uther?"
she asked him.

"No, I don't. I'm old and weak, now,"
King Uther told his wife, "and I can't leave
my bed. I know that I am dying, my dear,
but Merlin will help you, and he is **wise***
so don't worry."

When the wizard Merlin heard his name,
he came to the king's bed and sat with
Uther and Igraine.

Uther whispered, "Merlin, the time has
come. You must fetch our son."

*Definitions of words in **bold** can be found in the glossary on pages 63-64.

CHAPTER TWO

Do Uther and Igraine Have a Son?

The old king could see the other people in the room. There was his dangerous, clever **stepsister**, Morgan le Fay, with her son Mordred, who both practiced magic.

Uther closed his eyes. He was too weak to keep them open.

Then Uther said, loudly, "Our son will be the new king."

"Your son?" Morgan said. "You and Igraine have no son. My son Mordred must be the new king."

"It's time for me to fetch the boy," thought Merlin.

He could remember when, sixteen years ago, he took Uther and Igraine's baby, Arthur, to Sir Ector's castle. There, the boy was safe, far from Uther's castle where dangerous enemies were hiding. Arthur and Kay, Sir Ector's son, grew together like brothers. Only Merlin, Sir Ector, and the king and queen knew who Arthur really was.

"Uther," Merlin now said, quietly, "I'm here."

Uther replied, quietly, "Thank you, wizard. You have helped us through many battles against the **Saxons** and our other enemies— we trust you. Now, it's time for our son to be king."

"I'll look after everything," Merlin whispered.

Loudly, Merlin said, "Please, everyone, come to the stone near the church on Christmas Day. Everything will become clear."

After these words, the king never opened his eyes again.

CHAPTER THREE
Sir Ector Arrives

A few weeks later, it was Christmas Day.
All the **knights** and important people in the
country traveled to the church.

Kay and Arthur came with Sir Ector.
"We're old enough to fight great battles
with our father," they said as they arrived at
the church on their fine horses.

Suddenly, Kay shouted, "Where's my sword?"

"You can't fight great battles without your
sword, Kay!" laughed Sir Ector.

"Did you leave it at home?" asked Arthur.
"I'll fetch it for you," he said.

Arthur took a different path back to Sir Ector's castle. Suddenly, he saw a sword by the road. He stopped and took it. "Kay can have this fine sword," Arthur thought.

"Here you are," he said to Kay when he found him and Sir Ector.

"Where did you get this?" Kay asked.

"Yes, where did you get that sword?" Merlin asked. "May I have it?"

"Of course," said Arthur, "I found it by the road."

Sir Ector immediately recognized the wizard. "Merlin," he said, "do you remember my sons, Kay and Arthur?"

"Yes," Merlin smiled. He walked **toward** the church, carrying the sword and said, "Let's meet near the stone in one hour."

Chapter Four

The Sword in the Stone

All the knights and important people of the country were standing near the stone by the church. There was a beautiful sword in it.

"That's the same sword," thought Arthur.

"Men," Merlin announced, "only the real king of our fine country can pull this sword from this stone. Who can pull it out?"

The men came forward, one by one. Nobody could pull the sword out.

Two men wearing crowns tried. They had much land and were kings of their countries. They thought that they could pull the sword out, but they could not. Then, Mordred, son of Morgan, tried. He pulled and he pulled, but Mordred could not move the sword.

"Mordred is not the new king," everyone said.

Chapter Five

Arthur is King

"Perhaps my boys should try," said Sir Ector. Everyone agreed. Kay could not move the sword, so Arthur walked to the stone.

He put his hand on the sword.

Arthur pulled, and the sword easily came out of the stone. The sun appeared from behind the clouds as Arthur held the sword up above his head.

Merlin stood in front of the excited crowd and announced, "Countrymen and knights of this fine land, years ago, I took King Uther and Queen Igraine's baby boy to Sir Ector's home. Uther's castle wasn't safe—enemies were everywhere. So, here's your new king—Arthur, son of King Uther Pendragon."

The happy crowd immediately **knelt** in front of their new king, although Kay, Sir Ector, and Merlin saw Morgan and Mordred leaving quietly, with angry faces.

"I thank you with all my heart," Arthur said later to Sir Ector. "You'll always be like a father to me."

CHAPTER SIX

Camelot—A New Castle

The new young king was very busy.

"Arthur will lead us through these difficult times. Together, we can protect the peace," people said, as the Saxons and other enemies started attacking the country again.

Arthur built a new castle, called Camelot, to the west of Uther's old castle. From here, he could protect his country better. With his knights and soldiers, Arthur left Camelot to fight many battles.

Merlin and Kay stayed at the castle to protect it and the many people who lived there.

Arthur and his army often fought battles to help their **allies**. King Leodegrance was a friend and ally. When a strong enemy attacked his small army, King Leodegrance needed help fast.

Arthur and his men quickly reached a hill that was above the battle. They could see the enemy's many black **helmets**.

"The enemy are winning—let's go, men!" shouted Arthur, and they rode into the battle and helped King Leodegrance's army **defeat** the enemy. Arthur fought very bravely.

CHAPTER SEVEN

Arthur and Guinevere

That night, there was a big **feast** at King Leodegrance's castle. Here, Arthur met Princess Guinevere, King Leodegrance's daughter. He thought that she was the most beautiful woman in the land—and **fell in love** immediately. Guinevere also fell in love with the handsome and brave young king.

The next spring, Arthur and Guinevere were married at Camelot. There was a very big feast, and people came from everywhere in the country. They came from King Leodegrance's **kingdom** and other places—Uther's stepsister Morgan le Fay came, too.

Merlin knew that King Leodegrance was a good friend to Uther and Arthur, but he was not happy. He did not trust Guinevere.

"I feel some magic around this beautiful young woman. Why is Morgan here? Is this Morgan's magic spell? I must watch, and protect Arthur," Merlin thought.

Chapter Eight
The Round Table

King Leodegrance was kind to Arthur and gave him and Guinevere many wonderful presents. The best present was a big round table made of beautiful wood.

"This is for you, your knights, and your allies to sit around and discuss how to look after your country and protect your people," King Leodegrance told the young king.

"What a fine present," Arthur said. "All these important people and I will sit in a circle, so we'll be **equal**."

Soon, Arthur had regular meetings at the round table with his knights and with neighbors who were friends and allies. They wanted to work together to protect their kingdoms from enemies. They became known as the Knights of the Round Table. Each man made a special promise to Arthur and the other knights. "Together, we'll protect our lands and people," they said.

Merlin watched everything carefully. One night there was a big storm, and Merlin was worried. "Is this a storm," he asked himself, "or a magic message? We must be careful of our enemies."

CHAPTER NINE

Lancelot

"It's summer, we've defeated the Saxons, and there's peace in the kingdom, so let's plan a feast and a **tournament**," Arthur said to Guinevere.

The day of the tournament arrived. Many fine knights **dueled** well, but Arthur won every **joust** that he fought. Then, another knight arrived.

"Who's that horseman?" everyone asked. "Look! He might be a better horseman than Arthur."

Arthur and the horseman dueled bravely, but they were equal in skill, so the two men got down from their horses and fought with their swords. They both fought well, and neither man won.

"Take off your helmet, my friend," said Arthur. "You fight well, and you're the champion today. Who are you?"

"I'm Lancelot of Brittany," replied the man. "I'd like to be one of your knights and join the Round Table."

"You're welcome," said Arthur, and he made Lancelot a knight.

Merlin could see that Lancelot was watching Guinevere, and Guinevere was watching Lancelot.

"Hmm," thought the wizard, "I'll protect Arthur. Perhaps this is Morgan's work."

CHAPTER TEN

The Lady of the Lake

Later, Arthur showed Merlin his sword. "This is the sword that I love, and which I took from the stone . . . Look, Merlin, it's broken," he said, a little sadly.

"Don't worry, Arthur, this sword has done its work," the wizard replied.

Merlin continued, "This sword showed people that you are Arthur, son of Uther, and our new king. There's another sword for you, now. Ride with me tonight."

That night, they traveled together to a wild lake that Arthur did not know.

Merlin was silent as they walked through big trees that grew all around the lake. Then, Merlin put Arthur into a boat, which he pushed into deep water.

"The Lady of the Lake will meet you and give you a special sword," he said. "Take it, Arthur."

Suddenly, a woman's arm came out of the water holding a fine sword. Arthur took the sword, and the woman's arm slowly disappeared back into the water.

CHAPTER ELEVEN

Excalibur

When Arthur reached the edge of the lake with the sword, the wizard told him, "This sword is yours, Arthur. It will stay with you always. It will protect you, and help you to protect the kingdom. It is called Excalibur."

"Excalibur, you're the most beautiful sword in the world," Arthur whispered to his new sword. "Thank you, wise Merlin," he added. "The kingdom, its people, and the Knights of the Round Table will be safe for a long time with this sword."

Arthur and Merlin rode home through
the night. When they reached Camelot,
the knights said, "Where were you?
We were worried."

"Sorry," the young king answered. "We had
to go and fetch Excalibur."

"Excalibur?" they all asked.

"Yes, look! Excalibur is my fine new sword
that will keep us safe from enemies and
magic spells. Excalibur will help defend us
all—me, my young queen, Guinevere, the
Knights of the Round Table, and our lands."

The sun came out as Arthur held Excalibur
up above his head.

Activities

The activities at the back of this book help you to practice the following skills:

Spelling and writing

Reading

Speaking

Listening

Critical thinking

Preparation for the Cambridge Young Learners exams

1 Read the information. Choose the correct names, and write them in your notebook. 📖 ✏️ 💬

Uther   Igraine   Merlin

1 He is a wizard who can do magic.

2 He is the dying king of Britain.

3 She is the queen of Britain.

2 Read the sentences. If a sentence is not correct, write the correct sentence in your notebook. 📖 ✏️

1 It was very noisy inside the castle.

2 The king was very ill.

3 People knew who the new king of Britain was.

4 The queen wasn't worried about the king.

5 The king asked Merlin to fetch their son.

3 **Talk to a friend about the characters below.** 💬

Morgan le Fay   Mordred   Merlin

> *Morgan le Fay is dangerous and clever. She is . . .*

4 **Choose the correct answers, and write the full sentences in your notebook.** 📖 ✏️ ✪

1 There was the old king's dangerous, clever . . . , Morgan le Fay.

   a aunt   **b** mother

   c stepsister   **d** sister

2 Uther said, "Our . . . will be the new king."

   a brother   **b** daughter

   c grandson   **d** son

3 There, the boy was safe, far from Uther's castle where dangerous . . . were hiding.

   a enemies   **b** duels

   c guards   **d** knights

5 **Read the text, and write all the text with the correct verbs in your notebook.** 📖 ✏️

A few weeks later, it . . . (**be**) Christmas Day.

All the knights and important people in the

country . . . (**travel**) to the church.

Kay and Arthur . . . (**come**) with Sir Ector.

"We're old enough to fight great battles with

our father," they . . . (**say**) as they . . . (**arrive**) at

the church on their fine horses.

6 **Rewrite Chapter Three as a play script.** ✏️ ❓

The knights ride to the church.

Kay: Where's my sword?

Sir Ector: . . .

7 Look at the picture and read the questions. Write the answers in your notebook.

1 Who is in the picture?

2 Where are they?

3 What is in the stone?

4 Why do they want this?

5 Who can pull it from the stone?

8 Listen to Chapter Four. In your notebook, describe what's happening.

All the knights and important people of the country . . .

9 **Match the two parts of the sentences.**
Write the full sentences in your notebook. 📖✏️❂

1　Kay could not move the sword,

2　Arthur pulled,

3　The sun appeared from behind the clouds

a　and the sword easily came out of the stone.

b　as Arthur held the sword up above his head.

c　so Arthur walked to the stone.

10 **Read the answers, and write the questions**
in your notebook. 📖✏️❓

1　Merlin stood in front of the excited crowd.

2　"Here's your new king—Arthur, son of King Uther Pendragon."

3　Merlin took him to Sir Ector's home.

4　The happy crowd immediately knelt in front of their new king.

5　Kay, Sir Ector, and Merlin saw Morgan and Mordred leaving quietly.

11 **Read the questions. Write full sentences in your notebook, using the words in the box.** 📖 ✏️

> allies   castle   enemies
>
> helmets   knights   protect

1   Who was attacking the country?

2   What did Arthur build?

3   Who did Arthur go and fight battles with?

4   Why did Merlin and Kay stay behind?

5   Who did Arthur and his army help?

6   What could Arthur and his men see from the hill?

12 **Write a letter from Arthur to Kay at the end of Chapter Six.** ✏️ ❓

Dear Kay,
I hope all is well at home. Things are
very busy here . . .

13 **You are Arthur. Ask and answer the questions with a friend, using the words in the box.** ◯

> spring   kingdom   fell in love   feast

1 *Where did you meet Princess Guinevere?*

2 Did you like her immediately?

3 When did you get married?

4 Who came to your wedding?

14 **Write sentences using *Here*, *immediately*, *That night*, or *The next spring* in your notebook.** 📖 ✏️

1 . . . there was a big feast at King Leodegrance's castle.

2 . . . , Arthur met Princess Guinevere, King Leodegrance's daughter.

3 He thought that she was the most beautiful woman in the land—and fell in love . . . .

4 . . . , Arthur and Guinevere were married at Camelot.

15 Look at the picture and write sentences about it, using *Anyone, Everyone, Someone,* or *No one* in your notebook. 🖊 ❓

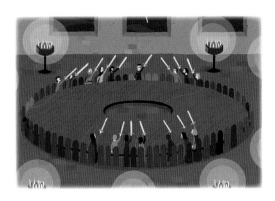

1. Everyone is holding their swords in the air.

16 Choose the correct words, and write the full sentences in your notebook. 📖 🖊 ⬟

1 feast	helmet	present
2 allies	enemies	stepsisters
3 duel	equal	wise

1 The best . . . was a big round table made of beautiful wood.

2 "This is for you, your knights, and your . . . to sit around."

3 "All these important people and I will sit in a circle, so we'll be . . . ."

17 **Read the definitions from Chapter Nine.**
Write the correct words in your notebook.

1   to beat the person or people who you
    are fighting   **d . . .**

2   people who were enemies of King Uther
    and King Arthur   **s . . .**

3   the country or lands of a king   **k . . .**

4   a big and special meal   **f . . .**

5   a competition between knights   **t . . .**

6   to fight in a competition between knights **d . . .**

7   a competition between knights on horses **j . . .**

18 **Listen to Chapter Nine. Answer the questions**
below in your notebook. 🎧* 📖 ✏️

1   What time of year was it?

2   What did Arthur want to plan?

3   Which jousts did Arthur win?

4   Who might be a better horseman than Arthur?

5   What did Lancelot want?

19 Complete the text using the words in the box. Write the full text in your notebook. 📖 ✏️ ⭐

is	Look	love
said	showed	took

Later, Arthur [1] . . . Merlin his sword.
"This [2] . . . the sword that I [3] . . . , and which
I [4] . . . from the stone. [5] . . . , Merlin, it's broken,"
he [6] . . . , a little sadly.

20 Talk to a friend about Merlin's plan. Ask and answer questions. 💬

How is Arthur going to get a new sword?

First, he's going to ride with Merlin to a wild lake.

21 Who said this? Report the statements below in your notebook.

Arthur   Merlin

1 "This sword is yours, Arthur."
Merlin told Arthur that the sword was his.

2 "It is called Excalibur."

3 "Excalibur, you're the most beautiful sword in the world."

4 "Yes, look! Excalibur is my fine new sword."

22 Read the text below. Find the five mistakes, and write the correct text in your notebook.

When Arthur reached the edge of the mountain with the sword, the king told him, "This sword is mine, Arthur. It will stay with you always. It will kill you, and help you to protect the kingdom. It is called Excalibur."

"Excalibur, you're the most beautiful sword in the world," Arthur whispered to his new wizard.

Project

23 In this book, you read about the Knights of the Round Table.

Find out more about one of Arthur's knights. Work in a group to make a presentation about them. Include the information below:

- What was the knight called?

- Where was he from?

- What was he like?

- What did he do?

- What was he famous for?

Glossary

ally *(noun)*
a person, or a country
that is a friend of
another country

defeat *(verb)*
to beat the person
or people who you
are fighting

duel *(verb)*
to fight in a competition
between knights

equal *(adjective)*
the same

fall in love (past
simple: fell in love)
(verb)
to begin to love someone
a lot

feast *(noun)*
a big and special meal

helmet *(noun)*
a hard hat that you wear
to protect your head

joust *(noun)*
a competition between
knights on horses

kingdom *(noun)*
the country or lands of
a king

kneel (past simple:
knelt) *(verb)*
to go down on one or
both knees

knight *(noun)*
an important man in
a kingdom

Saxons *(noun)*
people who were enemies
of King Uther and
King Arthur

stepsister *(noun)*
a girl or woman who is
the daughter of your
parent's new husband
or wife

tournament *(noun)*
a competition
between knights

wise *(adjective)*
clever, good, and
thinking carefully

toward *(preposition)*
in the direction of